P9-AFW-389

Fugitive Angels

FUGITIVE ANGELS

Poems by

Jeanne Murray Walker

DRAGON GATE, INC.

Seattle, Washington

1985

Grateful acknowledgment is made to the publications
in which some of these poems have appeared:

*Ariel, Ball State University Forum, Carolina Quarterly,
Chariton Review, Dancy, For the Time Being, Georgia Review,
Iowa Review, Kansas Quarterly, The Little Magazine, Louisville Review,
Motif, North American Review, Poet and Critic, Poet Lore, Poetry,
Poetry Miscellany, Prairie Schooner, Southern Humanities Review, Wheaton Alumni Magazine.*

This manuscript was completed with the aid of grants
from the Delaware State Arts Council and the Pennsylvania State Council on the Arts.

Dragon Gate, Inc. and the author thank the Literature Program of
the National Endowment for the Arts for grant support that aided
the publication of this book.

ISBN 0-937872-20-2
ISBN 0-937872-21-0 (paperback)
Library of Congress # 84-22984

First Printing
35798642

Published by Dragon Gate, 914 East Miller Street,
Seattle, Washington 98102

for Daniel

Contents

I

II

III

IV

I

The Butcher

On Tuesday afternoon a butcher wipes his nose and saws
a calf's hindquarter, fresh in from Iowa.
Like God, he knows the destination of each part.
He trims the fat for suet, whistling through his teeth,

thinking about a certain girl's red nails. He stacks
chuck steaks for Safeway, then loops his apron on its peg
and steps outside to smoke. Bending to tie his
rawhide bootlace, he hears tires squeal a block away,

and sees a woman from a doorway run to catch
a girl who wears a blue barrette, who's struck,
who lies, her ear and fingers curled against the street,
as though it were an uncle who would whisper

his last, precious clue to hide and seek.
The butcher watches cops collect like flies
then tucks his shirt into his pants
and pulls his door shut. He wanders a side street,

thinking of the picture by the peg,
pastel with age, curled by the summer heat,
the photograph a farmer sent from Iowa.
A hundred cattle low inside a fence.

He dreams of cradling one curly head,
to feed it nests of fresh grass and starflowers
which find their way to the most lovely places,
to long veins and complicated neckbones,

to the liver, bluish, slippery as wine.
Stepping into the picture, he leans against the fence

and moans. Above, clouds lower, gray as steel knives.
Hollows of eyesockets fill with blood.

He can't imagine any gods forgive like these.
Beside him goldenrods wave like children's hands.
All afternoon the butcher stands inside the picture
rocking one particular body in the mud.

Angels

– Ein jeder Engel ist schrecklich.
– RILKE

I. THE MOTHER

I will not send Susan away. She came
at a dark time when I was heavy
as a fly that drops in late fall.
I couldn't keep her clean. She couldn't talk.

But nothing else
suggested she was strange. No limp.
No stitches like rickrack lacing up
her head. Just eyes light green as spring leaves
focusing on an angel underneath the bed
when she was four. She ferreted out
clean angels from dresser drawers,
found angels with holes in doughnut shops
until Jimmy screamed, "No angels! No angels!"
But pointing at tables, at buses coming,
at my wrist, she laughed. She crooned their names.
When he was six, I found him in the den
pounding her temple with a tablespoon
to beat the angels out her other ear.
By now his arm has felt the brush of angels'
sleeves for thirteen years. He's learned their weight
against his chest. He understands they taste
like his own spit.

She's my best child. I cannot give her up. I need
to know she is upstairs, always upstairs
humming, a knife in hand, trying to free
angels for us, from little bars of soap.

II. SUSAN

When I saw the man through the keyhole
coming for me, a hundred angels
climbed down my back, rung by rung to my knees
and hid their faces.

"This will not hurt you,"
he promised, and laced me into white aprons
strong as appendicitis. He pushed me
out into a fever. In that noon glare
I was the only one who could not move.
I could not save my angels.
So they flew past my hand, pinned open
by my side. Smelling like rhubarb, their wings
stabbing sunshine like umbrellas, they broke
from me. I was the one left naked,
all of my dark joy gone. Translucent
as a fish whose guts have been scraped out,
the skin ripped off, the bones sliced out,
a fish whose body finally lies so luminous
you can see through it. I was invisible.

I learned to talk. After some time
they took me home. At first I stood in my old room
at the cracked window, trying to recall them,
trying to turn the gray stone by the sidewalk
back into angels. Trying to make an angel
of the dog tied on the porch across the street
where the stonemason dusts his pants at 6 PM.
I wanted my angels. I would have notched my bones
to make a ladder for their feet. But they
did not know how to come. Poor wings were lost.

Mother is dead. Jimmy has moved to Florida.
I learned from him that we were born to longing.
This is my house now, my window where I lean,

sometimes peeling the sash,
and say a short inventory of
what I know is true.
Prices go up. Someday an angel may lean near again.
I need a shampoo.

III. THE ANGEL

When her ribs cracked in the straitjacket
I popped out like a hazelnut,
naked and dizzy in sunlight, a broken angel.
The sun scraped my skin clean of hair.
It pried my hands open.
Eventually it shone through me
and the moon scrubbed my smell clean.
Then she forgot how foreheads can feel stars at night,
how knuckles can be bruised by wind.
She thinks now that stars and wind
are merely grit and motion.

There is no way to tell her
what she cannot hear or see.
I want her to feel angels in her lungs
like wood that stirs within the oak tree's memory,
sure of its end, hungry for the fire.
I want her to feel angels in her wrists
or eyes. For once
I want to see her eyes come true
while staring through me here
as I turn upon my lathe of air.

But she cannot feel the wind or hear me call.
My voice fades like the dying of a bell.
See how she goes deaf, cell by cell?

IV. THE STONEMASON

A young refugee angel stands in the rain outside
on the sidewalk. Can you hear her faintly crying,
searching for a place to scrub the stars
from her hands?

Well, let her in. Let her in.

But once she finds the water, will she find her hands?
She can't wash her hands unless we give them to her,
the hands with the good little scar on the thumb
and the fingernails blue from cold.
I'll make her hands. My wife will sew her gown.
My wife could pull the gray skin
from a rock and turn it inside out,
brushing off the warts and stitching it to fit an angel.
Angels have nothing, except on earth.
And earth's only magic arises from our need.

I need money. Suppose I chisel her
for good in stone, a headstone Jimmy will buy
in August when he is flush, when he is home
to see the grass above the place his mother lies.
I'll make the angel pigeon-toed, a shape the boy
will recognize. His mother.

V. SUSAN

I walk through wrought-iron gates
under a blue sky. Late afternoon. On my mother's grave
I toss a violent fistful of nasturtium
which will wilt in hours. I don't bend down.
A flaming flower catches on the angel's marble hand.
No one is here. I can see the clouds floating
in her eyes. I can feel her sleeves press
against my palm although I swear I try

to dangle both arms by my sides.
My thumbnail etches in her hair.
My knifeblade sculpts her cheeks. I smooth
her shoulders with my thumb.
Now she is rising
under my hands, freeing herself from the dead.
Lifting her eyes she looks at me until I too
begin to dream of floating
and she hands me
one orange flower.

VI. THE STRANGERS

Thirty miles down the red line on the map
from Johnson's Pond, telephone poles
rise like wooden garden rakes.
Pulling up beside a clapboard church,
a mother and child step into shade
where everything is furniture for the dead
who sleep so soundly they cannot raise
their doors to a child
who beats with staccato heels.

Wind skims above damp earth,
a high descant uttered by the tongues of trees.

As the temperature drops
the young mother hums a hymn she hardly knows
and watches the shining dead
who will not let her go,
stepping over their thresholds into marble.

She thinks:
O lovely pigeon-toed angel
cocking your head on stone for eighty years,

forgetting your dress, your fleeting thoughts
in the sleet of years
God himself cannot rescind,
our mouths all fail.
My child wears your fading smile.
My own words scatter in the opening fingers of the wind.

VII. EPILOGUE

The body someone took with love
has lain beneath this tree so long
that her last word is almost wrung
by wind from stone. On stone above,

a frieze of the angel she is now
stands changing her marble dress in wind,
growing fainter to its end,
the buttons losing place, the bow

untied to nothing, wrist refined
from rain to rain, at last to stone.
All a hand could touch is gone.
What remains is pure outline

of what she is, so light a shawl
that watching here, I think that I
can finally see her shudder, sigh,
and step into the marble.

Necessity

Trees are minimal in winter
as the x-ray of a hand
showing bones, ghostly, white
but indisputable.
Every day these bones suck sustenance
from water, meat and air
into long corridors
where they factor stories out.

Think of the stocking cap that waits
in some closet for a hand
to seize it. It may protect,
may warm against expensive cold,
but one day it will be delivered
to fire or garbage.

The bones say when.

Everything has brought them to this act –
birth, and food, and the chains
of swings in the playlot,
chains so cold we children
told how skin would weld on contact,
as it stuck with sweat
years later to other skin
we never trusted
but desired.

All our lives
skin comes and goes like weather
but bones are ghosts
which lurk beneath the skin

storing all our winters in their marrow.
They are like the fingers of snow-covered trees
whose shape we can't recall in summer,
the acts we won't believe in
till we feel ourselves
perform them.

The Witch: Jump Rope Rhymes

Prudence with your dirty dress
Fling your spoon and slap and cuss
Evil eye and matted hair
Wood and stake for your bone fire.

In a room without windows she sits,
left hand braceleting her ankle,
thinking at last of the fire,
for whom she arranges her face, her ankles,
to whom she will go soon,
her only jewels her fingernails.
For a long time she has been frozen
with a frost which cracks the brains of crickets
and hides the rivers behind death masks.

Wood and stake then light the match
Evil eye can evil catch
Ice for blood when she was four
Prudence killed her own mother.

How is it possible to become warm now?
Staring at a great stone in the wall
and the cement which will never let it go,
she wonders how to cling to the stake,
she who has never clung to anyone.
In these last clear moments,
as a spider walks across the red dirt
she feels her breasts grow heavy
and imagines the many open palms of the fire
holding her like the hands of many men.

Prudence killed a dozen more
Plague and flies and blood and gore

One skip two skip three skip four
Jump the rope till she's on fire.

She dreams that she cannot fall away
though hours later, when they come in
they cannot find a mark on her anywhere.

Making the Painting

I.

Like the criminal who waits across the street
for the nurse to snap the light on and undress
he sits before a Rembrandt, sketch pad on his knees.

She breaks from the umber shadow onto canvas,
the right plane of her face leaves dusk behind,
one earring dark, the other bright as a safety pin.

Straining her left shoulder forward, she gathers
amber light from his stare, her green gown
peeling away like ancient moss from new skin.

Skull neat as a cat's, her slender nose
cleared by the smell of turpentine, she craves him.
Their eyes lock into a beam between them.

Aroused to his feet, he stands peculiar for her.
His tee shirt's damp. His hands hang by his side,
ready for anything, veins blue as plums.

Then suddenly as though he'd found that Rembrandt
can be bettered, as though he'd taught the artist
how to see, he shuts his hands and strolls away.

II.

I exit, trying to find some meaning in this.
Maybe I am the woman in the picture. It dawns
how the blurred room came clear for the first time

as he stood there. Light. I remember now
waiting through dark years for his blue stare.
All that time I couldn't guess what I was waiting for.

But it comes back. Before he packed his sketchbook
and wandered off, he brushed a fly
from my shoulder. His hand felt curious,

lingering by the secret curve of collarbone.
His voice breathed slang that might have made Eve step
from air. And I remember someone moaned.

But no. We are like drunks, mistaking our own tears for rain.
We see ourselves in everything. Whoever that boy was,
we crossed looks only once, and in an art museum.

His shirt is clean by now and Rembrandts hold their value.
Those two will get along together or apart
without the likes of us. Come. Let's not think of them again.

Shopping at the Terminal Market in Dangerous Heat

The sun strikes, sharp against her car's hood.
By the intersection of Twelfth and Market, she downshifts
as a dazed bee stalls in air by the fruit stand.
The summer whets its blade on a tile roof and plunges
it to the heart of a dark eggplant. Sunlight
leaks out of peaches. In the air-conditioned car
she can't be touched by any violence of summer.

But she hears the green bell peppers ringing over
the noise of passing cars, the rasp of a hand brake.
Before she knows it, she is leaping out of her front seat
to snatch an apple and polish it on a pant leg.
She catches the hand and makes it lay the hot apple
back in its bin. Then she sees the fruit man's
steady gaze among the Idahos. Under his roof

onions are multiplying inside their jackets.
The spider plants are lowering their young by ropes
to hang like trapeze artists in the dangerous light.
Bananas elbow one another. This fruit man is stocked
with as many ideas as the ground has fruits and vegetables,
one idea for each shape, each shape safe to touch.
He holds a lemon up to let her safely watch the sun through it.

This is his idea, not hers. And she buys the shining fruit
in case someone she loves needs something luminous to eat.
The fruit man grins and snaps a brown bag open.
He drops the sun straight into the bag
through a hole in the air. Clutching it, she climbs back
into the front seat where she shifts into first
and turns toward home before the light can change.

Getting Saved in Molly's Drawing

While a cow staggers toward the left-hand margin
hurtling away from her tail
which hangs in air
and a wooba-wooba monster waddles after
jaws dripping with bloody limbs
shoulder stuttering ahead of his shaggy body

while cries arise from the cow
in shrill coils of graphite scribble
toward the sky
which is studded with dandelions
lying impotent
as so many dozing stars

while a grandmother hovers
over on the far right
imprisoned inside the receiver of a phone
forever trapped beyond the cow

the cow pauses
her ear speeding ahead of her body
and sniffs the sky

while the wooba-wooba monster gains
but
before it has finally snatched
one more body
undone
from one more drawing

the cow dreamily grazes a dandelion

which triggers a *rriinngg*.

The grandmother
hearing a star
is freed to spring.

Beyond Necessity: The Imagination

Place a bowl of strawberries on the table,
their erect hair and embossed seeds
still shimmering from cold water,
ruddy in the deep afternoon light.
You can eat them or not eat them,
transforming them to something else,
or allowing them to transform themselves
to something else.
No act is necessary but transformation,
which cannot be avoided.

Rocks can hold out longer than the rest of us
but go their own calm way to sand.
Feathers with their veins and
weeds with their portentous shadows –
to follow their changes, you must see
the world with an interpreter's eye,
always guessing toward change.

Hold things in the old hands of language,
the muscles of nouns and sinews,
prejudiced by pain and love.
With the hands of language you can grasp
the guide rope far into the darkness
like a silk thread
frayed but never snapping.

And in the final darkness
where language's lovely hands are empty,
you can hear the wings of geese
whirring like paper,
the sound of pages being torn from history.

You Make Your Own Luck

They're lost, the needle bouncing on perdition's side of red,
gas dwindling to a whistle in the tank,
that whistle dimming till it almost fades to fumes
and still the road, a stubborn prophet ranting
through Nebraska, foretells ahead of them
their prophecy: no town, no gas. Not one
flat board shack takes shape against the sky.
Then it doesn't matter what the names read
on their credit cards. They calculate:
the number of miles per gallon times the number of gallons
minus wrong roads they turned down, minus her bad luck
and his. They might as well be stripped of names,
of credit. Auspicious cornstalks clatter in the breeze
like bones. Three buzzards circle. Everything lies
grizzled by bronze dust. Between them they have plenty
of what they don't need, can't use: road maps
to everywhere, words sharp as razor blades.
She slides a look at him. He pulls the brake.
She writes in dust on the dashboard. He leans to read it,
asks, "Who wanted to come here?"
She doesn't say. Then he: "You happy now?"
"Don't tell me," she moans, "I know. I know."
The thought of getting out to walk makes
her brain limp. She thinks on all fours, like
a cornered animal, rubs her thumb for luck.
"Listen," he says more kindly, "a whistle."
She smiles. He tries the key in the ignition.
It starts. A car can't burn a smile. And it won't run
on his thin whistle. But they drift in
on that. They drift in on that. When they roll
into the valley, he grins at the gas jockey, says
"You pump your gas, Buddy, and I pump mine."

II

Street Magician: New Market Square, Philadelphia

The hippie squints, framing us
between his thumb and forefinger.

"I'm in charge of the magic show today
and you're the audience," he yells,
shaking his long hair like fireworks.

Two kids with open mouths plunk on the steps.
A man in a suit, a family of fourteen
drift in on the pizzazz.

"Want to see how to get an audience?" he asks.
"Applaud!" He wags a forefinger at us
and bows. He pulls a floppy hat from the air.
The crowd claps like loose screws rattling in a box.

He stares us down. "Got to do better than that."
He grins. We clap again. Thunder.

Blocks away, people lift their heads to gawk at him.
"Welcome to Cincinnati," he calls to them.

With hot pretzels in paper, babies in backpacks,
kitchen implements in crackling bags, they stream,
the skeptical, the shy, the rawfaced,
reeled in on a line of sound.
Like ants at the edge of a Kool-Aid spill,
we stand for the audience.

When he has us balanced
on his tongue's sharp edge, he says

"Want to see a hippie disappear?" He winks
slyly, sizing us up for the big lie.

"Shut your eyes." We shut our eyes.
He disappears, without even passing the hat.

Writing Stories in Philadelphia

You're a writer who's never sold a flower
writing a story about a woman on the corner
of Fifth and Walnut. She's hunched into her coat.
Suppose you set the woman in bleak winter,
hawking carnations. You let her finger
move to a gas contraption. You let it tinker
with burners till warmth caresses her face
like the Czech who loved her nineteen years before.

But her face is stupid as the frozen ground.
She recognizes no one. On her collar
dog-hairs wrangle; her nails are gnawed to blood.
The soles of her cardboard shoes lie down in mud.

Someone must force the woman to remember.
And so you make her grip a garden spade
in frozen hands to search out every corner
of an old plot.
The skull cannot be found,
although its shape – like a bulb – is so familiar
it could be anyone's. It lurks to spring
into her mind some random cold December
morning in the story, like a tiger or a lily,
like the face of her old husband, like a stranger.

Taking a Walk

She walks on Sunday afternoon into a park
which rolls impartially along, like a machine with golden wheels,

the sun strewing copper coins on children,
on shop girls, black baby carriages and old men,

each following a bright circumference, tracing
on ordinary grass the exotic curve of ordinary intentions.

How loosely the sun's heavy metal sits on them all.
And how naturally she begins walking toward the willows

bending over the river, their green stars touching water.
She is the parent of her walking and the child of it.

Beside the river she sees a statue, white as blank paper.
Down the corridor of willows, her thought bears the statue,

the pivoting feet, the blurring fingers, the drowsy face.
Her mind gestures in the center of everything, like this statue.

Suddenly the sounds of Spanish, French and Arabic rain over her
like loose nickels, and the woody voices of mallards clatter.

Although the dark metal of water puckers around white swans
it cannot harm them. She thinks how she has arrived

at polite agreement with everything, which she could always change.

The Construction Worker Thinks about the Woman Who Slept in This Apartment

The sound you hear is your wallpaper shredding off
the walls. I get paid four-twenty-five an hour
to walk through your old rooms and strip them bare.

I know you. You are the one who scratched *me llama*
Rosa Rodriguez on the bathroom windowsill.
Your slip lay like a ghost on the closet floor

the day they told me I was hired. Size 32.
I took it home. Now you are my ghost
whose Spanish nets my tongue all day,

whose plaster dust shakes down and settles on my hands,
whose empty kitchen cabinets feed me nothing.
At night the etched glass shade in your bathroom

is a peony I hold out to you. You touch it but
I see lights of an older country flicker in your eyes.
You turn from me, your forehead like a boat's smooth prow,

and I think of you standing in Havana on a dock,
the pilings pulled and sucked by waves.
You fished beneath a soldier's dead-bolt eye

until they called "Botes al agua!"
Then you jumped. Thinking of that when I am here,
I wipe the white film from your name to make it speak.

Across the street one of your little brothers
stands in the playlot where he learned kickball,

fingers hooked into the chain link fence searching for you.

You are not that one, you are not that one.
Are you that one, in the torn green skirt, stepping
over cobblestones, baby splayed against your back,
looking for new walls in a new country?

Tuesday Afternoon Meeting

What if, after coffee Tuesday morning,
our own geometry grows hugely clear:
like angles, we are committing ourselves
to a corner, converging in its shadow.

Then what is to be done? The appointment
must be kept. Suppose we send out reason
after the form: Can a syllogism
prevent the walls from meeting the floor?

You will take my hand and such love will run
between us as echoes in the mountains,
where two voices sound from one body.
It will become fiction that we were two

and equally fiction that we are one.
The corner receives the drastic angles
in pain and quiets their sharp differences
with shadow. With shadow it makes peace.

In these hours after thought and before act,
I regret having learned to count only
on my fingers. Yet, at last, we are the
corner. Can any counting pursue fact?

To Grandmother on Saturday Afternoon

Vacuuming the Sears blue and brown stippled rug,
stirring the lentil soup,
saving the stamps, then tumbling and stirring
at the five-o'clock edge of day,
staring at the paint-by-number sycamores beyond the walk
as the bitter wind tears the Minnesota dark.

You walked that dark behind a plow,
pulled taffy, pumped an organ,
sank in the days of your labor
to the depth of five children
and rose with your madness quelled.
No rage even to change your hairstyle.
A net careens over one ear.

You get up, goaded by a thought,
a pry, a twit of the minute.
To the whatnot drawer:
pencils, matches, nails, string bags, gum,
candlewicks, keys, radish seed.
Reluctant, cracked old fingers pushing,
pushing at the clutter.

Old crone, find it.
Find what you need.

The Aunt

When it rains, the aunt says
"I'm sorry," as though
by closing windows
she could have changed
drops back to moisture
inside a cloud
until I asked for rain.
My fingerprints still bloom
so flagrantly
on her doors and closets
that she could pick
and arrange them in bouquets
like dogwood in a mug.
Flying to visit,
she lugs my favorite muffins
in a plastic bag.
Even her floors
tilt in my direction.
My name clangs in her head
like church bells and
she puts me in the eye of God
three times a day at meals.
When I open mason jars
her dill reeks out.
Her mothballs
invade my clothes and
she drives my heartbeat
to heaven like an animal
she broke the hard way
long ago.
So I wonder why
I stand here at her bed,

doing nothing
when her eyes look final
as windows being shut
and locked
after the house she lived in
has been sold.

Measuring Distances

While standing in front of Huber's Sunbeam Bakery
she thinks of how the bus will pull up,
how she will grab the stainless steel post,
swing on, and how the bus will roll
from block to block over strange black pavements,
near chain fences, by weedy lots,
through scattered neighborhoods,
over the distance she cannot walk.
                                                            The distance
she cannot walk rises in the air like
the smell of the bread baking,
                                                    rises in her like
the quiet which fills her house when midmorning sun
fires the vase on the commode and the heating teakettle
ticks ticks ticks in the vast silence
which cannot be broken except by
the hand which grasps the doorknob and turns,
                                                                          the hand
which reaches across a distance she cannot walk.

The Uncle

By a certain shack where the waters of the Pacific
lap basalt boulders outside Lima, Peru
a little boy in a red-striped tee shirt

jounces stones in his wheelbarrow and sings
to keep them from drowsing before
the waves' endless ruminations on the shore.

No matter that his uncle who has lost him
halloos with despair through cabbages and brooches
against the daring glare of noon sun

far away in the open market, looking for his little suspenders.
No matter, for the boy is now squatting
on a boulder inclined above the ocean's jaws

and staring into the safe delicate face
of the sea anemone, which wants to turn purple,
and is turning purple for him

while over his shoulder, seabirds nest
in the shack which tends him like an uncle
falling to ruin with a gregarious grin of death.

Replacing a Button

The girl in the back yard, inching hand over hand
across a steel bar, her tennis shoes strolling in air,
her temple thrumming like a tambourine,

hears her own cells buzzing in her ears
the soft buzz a young girl always hears:
I'll never fall. I'll never picnic with gravity.

Go on, sapphire shadow. Creep across the leaves.
I can stay ahead of your cold edge.
The blue shadow creeps across a window

where her mother watches, narrowing her eyes with cold.
Over and over her fingers move the needle,
fixing a blue button on the child's dress.

For My Daughter's Twenty-First Birthday

I stroked her cheek with my finger
and she began to suck for dear life
like a fish in the last stages of suffocation above water.
When I poured my voice down to revive her
she grinned and graduated from college
Summa Cum Laude, schools of minnows parting before her.
"You are not a fish," I said to her.
"You are my daughter, and just born, too.
You should know your place.
At least we are going to start off right."
Like a woman whose hand has just been severed at the wrist
but who can still feel pain winking in the lost fingers,
I felt my stomach turn when she moved in her crib of seaweeds.
"Last month at this time," I said,
"you and my heart swam together like a pair of mackerel."
But she waved goodbye from a moving car,
hanging onto her straw hat with one hand,
light reflecting from the car window
as from an opened geode.
I wonder if she knows how I have stood for years
staring down through the fathoms between us
where her new body swims, paying out silver light.
It is as though I am still trying
to haul her up to me for food, for oxygen,
my finger in her mouth lodged like a hook.

Swimming in Dead Summer

Here at the water's edge where we lose our grip,
where we turn our skin over to the sun,
where the wind ruffles the hair on our arms like pages,
the waves answer: *Anything you wish.*

And I remember the unearthly story my daughter told
when she was eight, how she almost swam out of her name
in the blue water on the California coast.
She floated out to where the undertow

takes oaths to be impartial. It seized
and pulled her under with its murderous hands.
"I called and called," she said, "but no one came.
I swallowed water and when I had almost given up,

I felt bottom. And I survived myself."
Now in this mortal craze of sun I strain to hear
the waves, which mutter how we survive ourselves.

Wearing Sally's Gypsy Dress

– for Sally Hoffmann, 1937-1982
Middle States Women's Tennis Champion

Four months after you died of cancer
your mother, who kept my only daughter
for love, looked in your closet
and smelled the stinking breath of the black bear,
grief. "Sally's dead," your mother muttered
over and over to kill improbability.
She forced her tongue to keep touching the same molar
until the electric twinge was either gone
or permanent, all afternoon
folding dresses in the black bear's shadow.
She gave your denim to Little Sisters of the Poor,
sent your blue gypsy dress to me.
Mornings, I have drawn your dress over me
like water, waiting all spring to be rinsed
into a second life.

I never met you. But here in the side yard,
you step into me as into a ground stroke. Knees bent,
you teach me to follow through. I could run
far on these new legs, every muscle
a star that cannot be extinguished.
Pain's been packed up, sent away.
Sunshine lies durable on fallen
apple blossoms. Boughs shift, feeling
the new weight of swelling apples.
Iris quiver open, purple jaws whiskered
and fierce. Your pulse lobs
beneath my skin, *What's next?*
What's next? We lift the gypsy skirt,
step through the grass, smooth as a woman
going in to lunch.

The Walk

Last night I took a walk with him.
He tried to walk beyond his mother, I think. We stood
in the mud beyond sidewalks, beyond this rim
of light that holds the city in, beyond
the church, beyond everything. You see,
I went to him to try to make him talk
about death. Half my life ago
my father died – his mother, yesterday.
Our opposite parents. I thought he would know
the way the child in him was pushed away,
the need to make a world when the first womb is gone.
Creation – that's the point.

And yet
he helped her die. Her eyes were shut. She bled for weeks.
The doctors said she wouldn't make it to Wednesday,
then to Friday. Finally he took her hand
and said, "Go to Daddy." While he walked away
to find a nurse, she understood. She shut her hand
and died.

Look at the snow blowing north
across the ground. It's cold tonight. We should
have worn our boots.

Last night
it was as though he walked out of himself.
He said nothing. The way he walked said *misery.*
He took her misery so that she could go,
a kind of birth for her. But death for him.
He'll shut her in the ground. Is that birth?
Dead is dead.

And yet for him
pain seemed as natural as the notch
on that tree. For him bodies are the beginning

and the end and his only church
is his mind. He knows what animals know.
It was as though I watched the first man watch
his mother die. Remember that old hymn –
Miserere? Perhaps it's always been the sound
of blood pursuing blood, since the first dead,
through veins, through naves of muscle and around
the bruised, astonished altars of the head.

Well, tomorrow we'll send flowers. Yes, flowers.
But why can't I forget the way the darkness seemed
to gather in his marrow bones?
It seemed that in his eyes an old wind blew and sleet
freed stones. Old fires were built, old spears were hurled.
The pain of generations makes him complete.
He wouldn't talk. Perhaps he doesn't know.

But then why did it seem we were in another world
where the ground broke like water under our feet?

Northern Liberties

This time I am going to tell the truth about what happened
the day we drove through your childhood by mistake.
As you were shifting into third, you said, "My God,
it's Commerce Street," and there we were, idling in front
of the yellow brick house you lived in with your Jewish grandparents
and your young, crazy parents, the wrought-iron gate you climbed
still standing underneath the giant lilac bush.
The store where you bought caps was advertising religious articles.
Across the street, a Roman Catholic cathedral with pink marble pillars
and blue tile loomed holy as a witch's sugar house, selling novenas
on Tuesdays at ten. We turned the corner and drove around the block
following an arthritic trolley past the long-gone open market
with beets lined up on trays like the earth's skinned hearts.
When we came back to stare at the old house again,
the sun had shifted between buildings and shot us in the forehead.
The lilac breathed fire. I could see where you had fished for mackerel
from the second-storey window, where your pets lay buried,
where you dug a hole to China with a tablespoon,
where your Irish father leaned across your tart-tongued Jewish mother
with the improbable beauty of a tree turning in the fall.
In a minute the rose of Sharon spread all over your back yard like applause
and the door to old Mr. Greenhagen's house slammed shut again.
You shifted into first.
"Well, that's it," you said, looking at me.
And you pulled into traffic as though out of a dream.
I did not lay my finger on your wrist to stop you from going
anywhere you wanted, even to the place
we both now know is China. Time has already stopped
so many things you want. I will say nothing that is not true.
When I looked back, I saw, beside the lilac bush
which had turned its green and natural self again,
a boy running the streets of Northern Liberties into his feet,
looking for you.

The B Movie

At 9:04 on Thursday night, she watches him
flag the train with his umbrella.
The train slides to nothing. He climbs up the steps
to the platform of Friday, safe from her hands.
She can no longer touch his herringbone coat,
the buttons, or the sharp wool which blossoms beneath his coat.
His train pulls away, leaving her body imprisoned in Thursday.
She is locked in place like an old movie, reaching after him,
the same footage rerun, rerun, rerun
to the hum of old desire played on a broken comb.
She sits on a green park bench for a long time, her hands folded.
Poor hands, with veins crawling uphill
on their tracks beneath the sunburned skin.
Poor knuckles, which are no-man's-land.
Poor stranded forearm. Poor elbow crooked with love.
Poor heart that pulls its cars in the fog.
The train pulls out of the station repeatedly.
It is always Thursday and he catches it every time.

He Is Reading Abélard

He is reading Abélard with sunlight falling
on the lawn, on the old book, falling
through centuries onto the pure words.
In front of him, sunlight turns like a madrigal here
and here on the arbor's hidden grapes.
Behind him, sunlight is dozing in
the violent cracks which furrow the stucco wall.
Abélard's long desire descends from the old pages
like a cadenza pouring into his lap and he thinks

what if behind him now a door were opening?
What if a woman were leaning there, were stepping
down one step, light speckling her chestnut hair?
What if she were pausing by the wall to listen?
Then she might lodge her kitchen knife in one dark crack,
commit her basil to her dark apron pocket.
She might step over the lawn and stretch
her palm across him to find the fruit
which waits, swelling in the arbor.

If so, her arm would lay a long blue shadow like this
path obscuring the pure words in the book.

Transaction

Now I understand what these words mean:
mortgage, interest, fire insurance.
For years our only transaction
was your thumb pressing my thigh,
my mouth on your mouth.
A snarl of dark stars
was the roof over our heads
and your hands were my insurance.
In those days I wanted us
to own a house a long road down
from rain and hail
where imagination places
its street sign. Brick,
I wanted it, and fox-colored,
with stairs so easy to climb
they fooled the heart.
I wanted a front porch
where we could sprawl
hearing the sun sing like a brass choir
on window boxes filled
with flowers I could water.

Now I stand before these three steps,
holding tomatoes I can plant
in this back yard if I want to.
I close my eyes and listen
to someone's shoes climbing
onto the porch. Mine.
Someone's hands hold a signed contract.
Someone's hold a mortgage.
These are the figures: three

steps up and three steps down
most days of our lives to this house
which is blind, deaf, dumb
to any dream but being here
when we come. Someone's hands
are unlocking the front door.
Yours. We step in and shut the dream out,
forgiving one another.

Birthday Poem for My Husband

The day I was turning thirty-nine,
I couldn't see to read.
The letters dove for the margin
like escaping fish.
Having reached the best part of the story,
I had to close the book
and take a walk past the neighborhood
bridal shop and beauty school
where a school-aged girl hunched,
wearing a peasant blouse, looking old,
her hair stacked to heaven
and starched in place.
Traffic swam by, vicious as piranhas.

When I walked back in our door, I asked you
"How long do stories last?
When is the good part over?"

> "The Good Part," you mused.
> "A name for a beauty shop."

I frowned. You tried again.

> "A movie where people split
> but make the best of it."

For the rest of my life you will tell
bad jokes in good time.
In your language
the world might turn to anything.
Your tongue is like an Irish harp,
strung for all weather,

like an escaping fish which curves and flashes.
You are always in the center,
riddling for everything
you and the word are worth.
It doesn't take eyesight
to see what the good part is.

You play it slapstick.
You play for keeps.

Charm for a New House

In March the sun turned north, across
your kitchen table. By April may it unfurl
leaves of ivy to toss upon the wall
you look at every day. May weeds and moss
rage on the dormer below and may you take
the trouble to angle a look from where you sit.
Then may their lives damn all your fears to death.
May cats in heat howl briefly and one rung
lower on the ladder of desire if they sing
in your yard at all. May they never satisfy
their hearts' heat with birds. May everything
that prowls beneath your gaze live safe, live long,
and may you understand that their strengths lie
in them because you looked.

May what you see
within, your rugs, your books, your pictures, take
you welcome, into them. May the brown and blue
still life on your wall be still each time you look
in its own colors. May each thing come back.
May each be true, the keys, the shirts, each shoe,
your plants and spoons in their own shapes. And may
the blue stripe that circles your crockery bowl
charm it from flaws as this spell charms away
whatever can cause your heart to crack and fail.

Mother's Day Poem

On cold spring mornings my mother lugged
a wicker basket full of wash
up the steps from hell, her Boston terrier
padding behind, licking her legs.
As she stepped into sunshine
by the sandbox, crones in gingham
drew their noses toward their windows.
Aunt Evie stabbed her elbows to the sill.
Mrs. Aspic squared her arms,
clenched her sweater close to her fat ribs
and stared, while mother swabbed the rope line.
Her steaming rag ran the track
from Hazen's end to Tangalene's in fifty seconds flat.
Her breath became a long beard, a pillar of cloud.
She lunged to grab the napkins,
snapped them, strung them up taut
as the town square, the sheets,
the pillowcases, each item by its kind,
stripes with stripes, reds with reds,
each thing restored to its own shape
and filed in the precise air.
The rumpled sole of an old sock
she found sulking under the bed,
peeled it right side out, redeemed
and hung it by its toes.
The clothes stayed where she put them,
dwelling on the clothesline, whatever
the wind mentioned to the contrary.
Shadows sculpted seams, oh, in the rising swell
of wind, every towel and washcloth
went over and over itself,
breathing its own color back.
In a deep stack of ancient sunshine

each thread came to a greater knowledge
of itself. Then the crones sang "Hallelujah!
All order multiplies from perfect wash."

The small bones of the inner ear
tintinnabulate, "*Clean clothes.*" The hands
with their complicated opposing thumbs clap.
Knees rouse. All the mothers of the world
unpin the clothes and hand them to us.
They bend and flex. They fit.
We wear them in the streets like a creed.

Directions for Spring

– for Helen deVette

Watch the daffodils. Though they are not up yet,
already they are unstable, their high yellow
waving by the deep riverbed like a gang of suns.

Beware of how you plant them. Place the side marked
MADE IN HOLLAND down. Burn the box. Dig holes
at night and do not admit hope to your neighbors.

In winter, do not read Wordsworth, whose fields
permit riots of heat in the most implacable freeze,
whose breeze never stops shuffling pages of stamens.

Do not think of them in the dark, in basements,
while scanning the *New York Times* on the rise of crime,
or while making necessary arrangements with people.

Daffodils will take advantage. If one of them gets her green foot
into your last permanent room, nothing can follow but
bliss, crouching on every threshold, blocking all exits.

Should the strong arms of daffodils succeed in their terrible shove,
you will lose your last method of knowing sorrow:
you will recognize only love.

Prayer of a Wallpaper Stripper

For the swish of alyssum which grazed
like spume the gangplank of this walk
in the long pull of hot wind,
for the clouds which rolled this morning
on the hot sky like cool water,

for this house which hovers in the neighborhoods
of mimosa trees and tar,
for the door, for the walls
which will confess slowly the stripes and secret roses
of seven families in the halls,

for the black handle of the putty knife
which winks in my hand like a tiller,
sure as the star
that rode last night over the city
in the clean hands of the air,

for the knife's deep glide,
for the good path my scarred hands find,
I give thanks now
and for the contagion of wallpaper
which foams beneath its prow.

Colors

This Sunday Philadelphia cannot get enough of itself.
All its colors are flying on the parkway.

We know the flags by heart.
They celebrate our motherlands.

We do not need to squint into the sun this morning
or to listen while they snap our names.

We come to attention a dozen times a day
startled by the thought of our separate colors.

Beneath the flags you and I are taking a walk
to the boathouse on the river.

A boy in a green shirt glides by on a bicycle,
its spokes scribbling crookedly on the sunshine.

A child toddles too near the margin
where red flowers go over the edge.

When we get to the river all the silver boats are out
sculling through the water as if it were no work.

But it must be work for the hands.
And it is work for the eyes

to make a bicycle, red flowers, boats and a river
out of so many luminous specks

because there is nothing this city cannot pretend
with colors under such a wide open sky.

III

Making Change

I.

October in this town is bright with death;
the last red rags unravel from a dead
oak. And like balloons in comics, our breath
hangs in the air, as though what's said was said
for all time. If you were here, I'd say
Let's make some words that will unfreeze the air.
Let's set the alphabet on fire. Let's sway
like pyromaniacs until the bare
trees kindle. Let's dance till spring. Let's –

Enough. For love of you, I give some suet
to a tree sparrow and try once more to read
the news. Iran and oil. A columnist bets
we'll have to pay more to be warm. We'll do it.
We barter our lives away for what we need.

II.

Sitting here tending the sour fire
of need is crazy. I can't tell which part
of you is real, which part I madly conjure
out of smoke. Knucklebone and heart?
Shoeleather? Callus on the thumb? Are you
or were you ever double-jointed? What
kind of toothpaste do you use, and do
you wait to cross until the corner? Shut
the door. Read on. I've never met you,
or met you fifteen years ago. You feed
the pigeons. You're my father. You are you.
Whoever, keep me warm and I'll admit
this once, it's you with whom I must exchange.
But still, I rhyme on foreign. You on strange.

III.

The leaves' enameled reds burned to bronze heat
in half a day. Too much fire too fast
is worse than not enough. My child's feet
tap Jingle Bells. What's past is past
redemption. The future's marked with your
absence – vivid everywhere as bows
on Christmas presents I buy you earlier
each year and cannot send. My hand still knows
your matted chest. My hair still webs your fingers.
Only I can't remember: when we wrestled
knee to knee, locked in such fierce caress,
were you companion or enemy? Strangers
come caroling to warm me. My child sleeps, nestled
in what may save us yet. Another Christmas.

IV.

It's winter solstice evening. I have gone
defeated to the city. Night will yawn
luxuriously on for lovers who
tramped little shops at noon, and laughed at 2,
tinseled the tree, crossed looks, ate shellfish, locked
an early door. And drink to jazz or rock.

Suppose behind one door, on the maroon
divan the tall one contemplates the moon,
broken again this month. Beneath his shirt
his heart makes little staggers. He's hurt
or he's in need. Her shadow cuts
the light beside him. Watch them. But
I'm outside and every door is locked. The blue
air turns to night. I drag the streets for you.

V.

Christmas came and went. God can be silent
when you and I would break. For weeks the baby
lay in his crib beneath the blinking, violent
colored lights, beside the crèche's shabby
kings and shepherds, straw in his mouth, intent.
Outside, birds bruised their wings on brutal air.
I found a dead sparrow. What Christmas meant
escapes me now. Papier-maché and wire.
Except I have learned this: that everything
with feathers has to quarrel to gain height.
You are the air I beat my wings against,
the bass whose descant I am forced to sing.
God bless our acts, we argue in the night.
May dark give way before our impotence.

VI.

Who needs astrologers, since I can check
the zodiac of air? I feel cold enter
on the axle of the turning oak,
standing in the circling months' calm center.
I saw you, yesterday, cross at the corner.
Traffic stood for the light. Then gears meshed
and engines turned again. I thought of fire,
for wind inscribed its sting upon your flesh.
Ice was legible on your bare hand.
Since warmth was driven out, a silent hermit
from our dark streets, into another land,
we either burn or freeze. The cruel climate
of need does not relent. And every breath
we draw leads, *ipso facto,* to our death.

VII.

Green is the new game. A bumblebee
hums a while to calm itself beside
a rhododendron. This fertility
will bring the summer. Those who need warmth collide,
lascivious with hope, and fire leaps up.
The lean tree spins. Sparrows shinny to heaven.
The axle turns until bright leaves heap up.
Contrive your longing now to learn abandon,
my lovely dear, and welcome back the hermit.
The bumblebee drinks at a scarlet flame.

My child cartwheels toward me. *Hurry, you're it.*
For what? I ask. She says, *It's a new game.*
It's one you have to pretend that you don't know.
OK, I say. *I don't know. I don't know.*

Physics

The doors of the long semitrailer truck
swing shut. A kid stands on the dock,
easing off his gloves, watching the tires roll,
hearing the engine grumble as it leaves
for one of those flat middle states,
dragging a hundred cardboard cartons labeled Grief.
Turning, he smears his red face with his shirt
and hoists another carton to the jaws
of another patient truck. His arms
are levers. His legs uncoil like springs.
In this gray town where houses are devoured
by ravenous black slate hills they cannot help
but cling to, grief is everywhere.
It rises out of chimneys, smelling like woodsmoke.
It airs its mug on new TV serials
and tackles his skinny brother
playing kickball in the vacant lot.
It settles in the blackened shack
that crazy William set on fire one night.
It crowds out asters like quack grass
and lifts its leg at the fire hydrant.
In prayer meeting grief scuffs its boots
on the pew it kneels by.

The kid

can't ship it out of town fast enough.
He swings his long legs over the dock during break.
They dangle weightless in a blaze of light.
He thinks about the only physics he has seen:
the love that bonds all elements
in their perpetual dance is grief.
He won't believe it, because he knows
how it might feel to sail over the rim of houses
into light. There nothing is held down

by the black fist of gravity.
Beyond the dock, beyond the roads, beyond
the tarpaper roofs, beyond the stubble fields,
seething on the horizon, he sees,
brilliant as a burst vein in his eye,
a light that will not go away.
He blinks and blinks but it stays, as though
it were the lever to lift the city by.

Why the Kid Failed to Commit a Murder

He cut the paw off a live cat
with a meat axe when he was ten
and she dragged pawprints through the flat
until he watched her stagger. Then

he cleaned the amber rug and tossed
her in a plastic bag from Sears.
Wishing he had not cried and lost
his dinner or his stolen beers,

he dabbed his mouth on his fouled sleeves.
But flesh adheres to its own laws.
Icy plans the mind conceives
may fail because the body thaws.

His flesh was always first to go.
Skinny, pimply, vague as drizzle
with facial tics, an itch below,
he wiped his nose on a long sniffle.

His smile bent in a treacherous crook
from years of swallowing by rote
because his mother knew a look
that rammed his laugh back down his throat.

Odd that he should now be booked.
The gun fell from his two-bit fist
because the waitress's wet hand looked
like his mother's fingers, his mother's wrist.

The Patient Finds Relief, Confessing to a Turtle

On Saturday morning
sun stings her eyes like medicine drops
while the matron laces her sneakers for the picnic.
Later, when they leave the bus, she runs
alone into the desert where she finds
a live sand turtle. She sneaks the file
from her purse to notch his shell. She hacks
a mark for stealing old Renzetti's cookie samples
then swearing by her mother's veins
that she did not.
Another notch for practicing off-key
on purpose.
For ruining new Mary Janes by wading in the mud.

For ramming her older sister's bike into the step
until its front wheel jammed.

She saws one for the day she sassed her mother
and her father shook her till the lights went out.

Notch one. Notch two. Notch three. Up to thirteen
and then she wanders off.
They say the turtle
sometimes bears his shell three hundred years.

Waiting in Slaytonville, Delaware, for God

Scuffing his feet on the worn floorboards, he unlocks the door
and enters the dark rooms. Things wait for him inside;
a redwood bed with imitation braided rope
looped on its headboard. A dresser with tilting mirror.

A Bible bound in oilcloth, open to Leviticus,
the chapter on abominations. On the sink beside the bed,
a Brillo pad and rubber gloves. He switches on the light,
drags a chair to the table and sits down to wait for God.

It's two o'clock on Sunday afternoon. A floorboard creaks.
He makes his eyes stop gazing at the cabbage-colored walls.
He makes himself look at the light that stands above the table
hoping to stare down the brilliant nothing that is God.

He thinks into the light. He strains forward,
trying to detect the quiet which can be to him
anything it wants. Lint rises in the yellow shaft
the way his mind floats as he listens into silence.

When Mrs. Cranford shuffles through the common hall
in bedroom slippers, he turns the woman from his mind,
leans farther into the dangerous air before him on the table.
He sits for hours and hours. Light moves from north

to south across his eyes. He gets up once,
stumbles to the toilet. He doesn't eat.
He doesn't even think about the cheese waiting
for him in its hard wax skin in the icebox.

He wants to know God's will. He turns himself into desire,
ardent and unquenchable until he hears
light steal across the scarred oak table
like a chain which finds his wrists and then snaps shut.

Waking Up in a California Correctional Institution

Every night at sunset, dust settles in his throat,
doors bang shut and lock, his mother climbs
into his eyes, sets fires of poverty,
and old thirsts tear his hands
until he dreams he runs, stumbling on
the stone beam of headlights and cars pulled in a ring
like six closed gates.
                                        The Doberman
who guards him whines like a rusty hinge
and measures ground beside the sandstone wall.

Beyond the dog, the sea eyes him.

He shutters himself against the sea
the way you'd zip a jacket
to salvage dwindling heat.

But he hears the sea
muttering in the chambers of his ear.
Waves forever lapping at basalt,
basalt forever holding against waves.

A Doberman can't guard such dangerous balance.

One day in July the waves break through the wall.
That night he turns in sleep.

Stretching, he opens his eyes
to see light pouring into his room

like the glint of water inching up the sides
of a new glass.
Blood pounds after good blood.
His cells press back against the amber air
and his skin holds firm against the snarl of the sea.

Rain Ritual of the Divorcé

A jealous lover, who somehow found
her new address, is stomping up the walk,
yanking open the door,
peeling off his mackintosh,
ransacking the furniture like a sheriff.
He feeds the cat to the spaghetti machine,
blinds the light
and murders the green peppers.
He uncorks the Chivas Regal
and pours it down the sink.
The sink unclogs.
The house shifts on its footings.

He sits down, pulls the nail
out of his shoe and rests
his curly head in his lovely hands.

The rains begin to fall
like a dozen women sighing.
His look is the cool cloth her mother
wrung and laid against her forehead
when she had chicken pox.
Cracks in the earth reknit.
Lilies of the valley hold up their cups for water.

"I don't know what got into me," he says.
She murmurs, "Nothing, nothing,"
and throws the windows open.

Flo's Song

I can't carry a tune, Bill says,
because my mouth is so small. Out here
it's nothing but snow and no dog tracks.
So many bits of snow falling through the air
there's no number for it. Snow in March
and me walking to a job:
swabbing floors all morning with Glo-Coat
and scrabbling with the venetian blinds.
If it weren't for bad luck
I wouldn't have no luck at all.

I left the house this morning singing.
Try to bone a song. You'll never
get rid of the splinters entirely.
But it's song in a cold March, never mind.
Angels are putting their bodies down in the streets
and fire leaping right up from smokestacks
like souls out of God's second coming.
I may fall down under the load before summer
but I got no room for complaints.
March, you give me the best days of your life.

The Students Bear Knowledge into the World

"So long," we say to our students.
They turn and wave. "Wish us luck
in the real world." Robes slough off their shoulders
the way protective skin shrivels from an iris bud.
The students bear new knowledge
across the mall in courteous hands.
Their tennis shoes bisect the campus.
They have become logicians.
They step on sidewalks carefully,
trying to keep off the finished grass.
Beyond the mall they go,
wading deep into final sunlight.
In front of them their shadows stretch.
See how the shadows hook and haul them forward?
They pass the last, legible hedge.
They pass the last stone wall, marveling:
How separate each brown stone stands.
How self-contained.
"Goodbye, good luck," we wave and turn.
Let them find the real world, we mutter.
May they all see the iridescent bottle fly preen
and hear one screen door bang repeatedly.
Let Greg, who has stared all spring
at the blue veins of Sally's instep,
understand that he wants all of her.
Let Sally stop writing fragments and say yes.
Let Ursula's long nose not matter for anything
but breathing. May Dennis's bum eye
not keep him from seeing what Plato meant by light.
We walk toward the sun, our voices
far away and finished as dried tempera.

Reading James Wright, Spring, 1981

One pony still stands where you put it
in this field, arching her throat
over the barbwire fence. Far in the distance,
finished with that throat, you stand.
You walk over the delicate green skin of the field,
grinning, waving, scratching your head, your wrist.
Your shoulders still seem too big for you.
You are solid as a salt lick on the little knoll.
If you lifted your deep voice, the whole field
could break into blossom. Only you
would not.
                All winter we have heard the little hands
of slugs, parsing the rich soil
beneath the locust trees,
                                        and angleworms
swimming, fathoms deep in loam, to warmth.
We harried this ground all winter to find one good
morning when we could hear you reason with them
in your plain voice. And now you stand here.
Over tufts of coarse sweet grass
                                                  you lift your voice
the way your brother's pitchfork in Ohio might lift hay
and hold it up to sunlight one spring morning
when the lawn is strewn with dandelions
giving back their fire to the sun.
You lift your voice across the field.
In your good time you say, *Good morning.*

Betting in Bright Sunshine at Delaware Park

– for Rick Smyth

He leans against the fence where he can see
long shots parade beside him to the track:
Calamity, Jay's Boy, Timbucktoo.
Grabbing a pen, he figures on his pass.
Numbers spin like women in his head
and while he handicaps, the crowd grows still.

The sun flips like a coin up in the still,
white sky while he adjusts his eyes to see
what he'll recoup this race. Glare splits his head.
She left like moonlight gone. He can't keep track
of why or what it means. He lets that pass.
At least he doesn't have to bet for two.

Until the fanfare shakes out flags at two
he figures: Even odds that she will still
come back. Satisfied to wait and see,
he scrambles off to watch the new field pass.
One moons at him like a young cousin, head
as dark as rumor in the paddock. The track

is fast, her name is Comeback. He keeps track
of her sweet swerve with one good eye and runs to
lay his paycheck on her gorgeous head.
Lord, he needs something finally to stand still.
He'd like to close the track tonight, to pass
home to a wife as true as middle C.

We bet the way we have to bet. The sea
of nags rolls off and he begins to track

her on the flat, the curves. He sees her pass
the roan, the chestnut mare, until she's off to
Jesus, kneecaps flying to heaven, still
true, still on track. The jock gives her her head.

Rags shaken in the wind, her mane. Her head
eats light, drinks furlongs. He can't even see
the blur until the photo. There she's still,
and first. And his. He rises beyond the track,
beyond his hands, his rings, his blue tattoo,
his shoes. The crowd divides to let him pass.

He floats above us like wash still blown ahead
of its own sleeves. We see him pass the track
to somebody's bare arms, bare hands, sweet back.

Ravinia, June 27, 1981: *Verdi's* Macbeth

–for Larry and Juanita Brook

Nothing exactly like this has ever happened before.
We have come here to recall the story that never changes,
we, who are going to die, who have already paid
with the small change of the lucky
to see how Macduff lost all his pretty ones,
how Macbeth then lost himself.

Three women stroll past. One wears a violet toga
which hangs like wisteria to her knees.
They go across the grass to the little table
laid with a red-checked cloth and white bone china.
Nails shiny as pebbles, they spread pâté on French bread.
As though she had just thought of how to make her throat beautiful,
one woman throws back her head and laughs.
The one sitting on the red plaid blanket picks up a plum.
Her silver teeth flash. Fixed to the trunks of giant oaks,
spotlights begin to blink on, all over the park,
and the great foamy heads of trees
float over us like unearthly props.
Back and forth people glide in pairs, as though miraculously
they desired to go where the script had planned
for them to be. A father steers his daughter by,
hand on her neck. Lovers in khaki shorts meander,
their hands in one another's pockets.
Another pair of lovers ambles without touching.
Three men are joking; their slang sings clear
as the smell of apples beside the little fountain,
where a bronze boy dances, kicking up skirts of water.
A slender woman wearing little sandals waves to someone
and reaches to accept a glass of wine.

The ushers, in uniforms which are new for the last time,
grow tense, lean forward, inhaling purple air.
Suddenly the voice of Sherrill Milnes plunges
like a dagger, stabbing the dark again and again.
Beneath the trees, before we can compose ourselves,
the woman in the toga locks her teeth midbite,
the men's mouths fall, the lovers link their arms too late.
The music comes for us, murderous and beautiful.

The Last Migration: Amherst, Massachusetts, Winter, 1981

– for Stephanie Kraft

The last shred of light falls on your wrist
like gauze. You lean at your hall window
to hear the hemlocks tossing in the wind
– old women, ankle-deep in shadow
now, and wading deeper in. The dark ground
is glazed with ice. Winter's come early.
Hardly any sunlight bandages your hill's
steep cold.
                    The birds that nest
in those old skirts should pack
their heads beneath their wings. Enough,
to dream about a burst of golden seeds
and summer in some place the sun finds
health. It's too late to fly south.

Your eyes watch them settling like lost hopes.
Everything must have some ending.
You recite their names: *geese,*
starlings, swallows, vesper sparrows,
and in this ceremony you are either accurate
or sorry. You are both.
                                        You get it right.
Truth is the thing you pull around your shoulders
like a shawl against the human chill. By incantation,
like sunlight on the tongue, you name them.

As though they hear, they part the air
with beaks as dark as liver. Slow,
puffed out like foam, losing heat,

circling, they swoop, and almost stall. Then rise.
Look. For all the weeks they need,
some knowledge in their ribs will search
like lanterns the dark way they have to go.

Turning from the window, you pull
your sweater close. Through cold they drill
for those unlikely homes that you could name:
Peru, the Carolinas, Tennessee, Mexico.

Coming East from Cleveland to Philadelphia at Harvest

– for Deb Burnham and David Staebler

I. SUNRISE

In early morning east of Cleveland, blue fog rises from hedgerows
and pasture grass ticks beneath the sun. Cows stare
with astonished eyes at the line where trees stave the horizon.
Like points of scarves, their ears stand out.
Their skin drapes over great wooden bones.
Their splendid cuds move from stomach to stomach.
Their milk leaks onto the small white flowers of strawberries.

II. ALLEGHENIES

Beyond the trees, the Allegheniess rise from land
sifted and sorted by the wind five million years,
the great shelves of granite wandering through the continent,
sailing their troubled prows up through fathoms of loam,
heaving their load, all scars and calluses, all whisker and hurrah.
A bridge threads the eye of the highest pass.
Tall clouds bear water in their hands
to streams which jangle their bells against rocks
as they swell and rush down grooves of land toward the Mississippi.
A violet rock shears loose, roars and crashes to the valley.
Three horses brace their ankles to stare
while a hawk spirals down with open talons. The grass squeals.
Plunging their necks into the long grass, the horses feed again.
They browse in their own shadows. They walk into the mountains,
reading the hieroglyphs of grass.

III. CROPS

Fat bales stud the broken fields.
In their secret places on the bough, apples swell.
The complicated seeds within get ready for their work.
Bees fill cells with heavy amber.
The corn works toward plenty, its kernels fattening,
its hair tasseling above cracked soil and singeing in the sun.
The leaves of the wild pumpkin sprawl, broad as open palms.
Everything is finished: pumpkins, pinecones, pods, nuts, acorns,
turnips, potatoes, carrots, beets, parsnips,
the roots have taken their days to gather starch.
Rings have slipped down the fingers of the purple vetch.
And the dry grass, silver-green, black-green, yellow-green,
waits for the final plow to turn it back to soil.
The redwing blackbird flickers, a heart beating in the wheat.

IV. WATER

In the lake, silent fish collect, their flesh packing close as
petals of a peony. A frog blinks on a salmon-colored
stone, algae multiplying between his toes.

V. THE BOOK OF ANIMALS

A girl in a Pennsylvania haymow reads the book of animals out loud.
Her limbs are long, her hair a bowl cut of sun.
This is what she sings to herself:

Praise the toad who pulls his bottom eyelid up.
Praise the thrush who ties his song like a bow in the air.
Praise the slug who carries rocks on his back.
Praise the mice who spread in the cornfield like laughter.
Praise the vulture who dips his beak into the deer.
Praise the skunk whose nose surpasses all others.
Praise the jackal whose blood buzzes behind his eyes.

Praise the perch whose bones are clean as pearl.
Praise the squirrel who stuffs his cheeks and prays with his paws.
Praise the possum who collects heat from the sun like a brown stone.
Praise the duck who pulls up her feet and rises into air.
Praise the fox who grins in the forest.
Praise the chicken whose head goes in and out like a piston.
Praise the snake who glitters in the black heart of the mountains.
Praise the hedgehog who listens with his inner ear.
Praise the humpbacked pig who roots in gold manure.

VI. SUNSET

While rivers engorge and flow toward the Atlantic,
while lovers nuzzle and mate in hooded nooks,
while freckled eggs wait in coops beneath yellow hay,
while wolfpups hone their teeth on the rabbit's thigh,
while sheep trot home in a line beneath their bags of wool,
while seeds crowd and split their husks,
while young foxes wander from their nests,
while gray stones grow heavy with lichen,
the sun hauls the gold and green land behind it
and shadows drag toward autumn,
the earth tilts once more on its axle
and each thing leans toward its own redemption.

Canning and Freezing the Crop

Anything memory squeezes
through the sieve of time
is fine enough to last forever.
The screen door bangs shut.
In the side yard, Richard's shucking corn,
his hands so perfect
sun gives light to them like an endowment.
Knees wide apart,
tin bucket between his legs,
he combs silk bangs out of the yellow eyes,
bangs the yellow out of the long ears,
and glances at the swing where his sister
eases her shoes on with a spatula.
Inside, their mother hums some music
to the old words, Waste not, want not,

pestles berries through a sieve
with her left hand
and with her right
pours paraffin over jelly.
Wind bangs the screen door shut.
One saves the vegetables, one saves the fruit:
any two points make a straight line
in geometry. In life nothing goes straight.
A monarch flutters dizzily
and falls like a bloodleaf.
Fall is coming early. Put this through your sieve:
Richard dies of booze before he's forty.
We preserve what we are able.
The screen door still bangs shut:
Waste not.
Want not.

Cover photo of Jefferson County Courthouse
architectural detail by Mary Randlett
Photo of the author by Eric R. Crossan

Designed by Tree Swenson
Galliard type set by Accent & Alphabet
Manufactured by Thomson-Shore